STIRRING UP TROUBLE

CHRISTIAN COZY MYSTERY

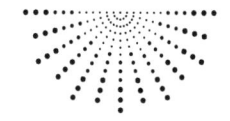

DONNA DOYLE

Publisher's Note: This is a work of fiction. Names, characters, places, and incidents are a product of the author's imagination. Locales and public names are sometimes used for atmospheric purposes. Any resemblance to actual people, living or dead, or to businesses, companies, events, institutions, or locales is completely coincidental.

© 2021 PUREREAD LTD

PUREREAD.COM

CONTENTS

1.	Hope for the Homeless	1
2.	Movie Night	9
3.	New in Town	17
4.	Unexpected Chaos	31
5.	The Grand Tour	39
6.	Preparing for the Worst	47
7.	Hoping for the Best	55
8.	Detective Sammy Baker, On the Case	67
9.	A Crucial Interview	76
10.	New Evidence	83
11.	Closing Arguments	91
12.	A Dose of Honesty	100
	Other Books In This Series	105
	Our Gift To You	107

1
HOPE FOR THE HOMELESS

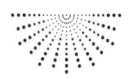

"They've finally reopened Thornton Street." Sheriff Jones sipped his coffee and then stirred in a little more sugar. "Now that we don't have as much snow on the grounds, the road crews were able to get in there and repair it."

"Good," Sammy replied, sipping a mug of coffee of her own. Just Like Grandma's was slow that morning. Some of the regulars were in, but they'd all been taken care of. "Now I won't have to avoid it on my way to work."

"You still liking your new house?"

"Oh, yes!" Sammy had moved out of the apartment above the restaurant just over a month ago and purchased a house on Poplar Street. She'd gotten very lucky with both the price and the condition of the home, and the previous owners had even included all their furniture. "I'm still working on making it my own. I've swapped out some of the prints on the walls, and I bought a few new knickknacks when Chelsea and I went shopping. I—"

"Sammy!" The front door of Just Like Grandma's whipped open, admitting the town's most prominent lawyer. Rob Hewitt was dressed in his typical attire of a fine blue suit, with his gray wool coat thrown over it, but he definitely wasn't acting distinguished as he barreled through the restaurant to the counter.

Sheriff Jones leaned away from him in surprise as he slapped his hands on the counter. "Sammy!" Rob was still shouting. "You'll never believe the phone call I just got!"

"I suppose I won't, unless you tell me about it," she replied with a laugh. "What's going on?"

"I just got a call from Rudy Rush, the campaign manager for Stephen Montgomery. *The* Stephen Montgomery," he emphasized.

Sammy was off her stool in an instant. She grabbed Rob's arms as excitement built in her chest. "You're kidding! What for? Why?" So many questions bubbled up that she didn't know where to start.

"A buddy from college is his lawyer now, and when Montgomery was looking for places to head out on his campaign trail he recommended Sunny Cove. I'm to make all the arrangements for his speaking engagements while he's in town, and he's coming next week!"

"This is amazing!" Sammy squealed. "We've got to make preparations! Oh, but I don't know the first thing about hosting a gubernatorial candidate."

"You don't have to worry about that. We just have to provide the venues, a little bit of hospitality, and arrange for a hotel. His campaign manager will take care of everything else." Rob's cheeks were still pink, and it was no longer from the chilly air outside. He was just as excited about this as Sammy was.

"Now, hold on just a second," intoned Sheriff Jones in his best voice of reason. "Are you telling me that a man running for governor—who also happened to be a major movie star back in his day—is coming to our little town?"

Sammy had nearly forgotten Jones was sitting there. In fact, she'd forgotten about everything around her except the idea of Stephen Montgomery. "Yes! Isn't that amazing?"

"Not really." He sipped his coffee again, a sour look on his face.

"Why not? Don't you see what a big impact this could have?" Rob grabbed a seat next to the sheriff, his blonde hair wild. "Stephen Montgomery is obviously very well known, and he's chosen homelessness as his primary issue to attack during his campaign and—hopefully—his time as governor. My lawyer friend told him about the work Sammy and I have been doing to try to create a homeless shelter, which is exactly why he wants to come here."

"And," Sammy added, "this might just be the kick in the pants our fundraising efforts need. We've pulled in some money for the shelter, but it's hard to get a large amount when you're talking about a small town. People tend to think they don't have a lot of extra cash lying around. Montgomery just might change their minds!" She could just imagine the change this could have on their little community, and her heart soared once again.

"That shelter is going to be a huge deal for our homeless community." Rob hadn't lost the tiniest bit of his enthusiasm, still evident as Sammy handed him a warm cup of coffee. "We've been doing everything we can, asking businesses and churches to be on a rotating schedule of warming shelter, hosting dinners here, but that's nothing compared to a real place for them to go!"

Sheriff Jones waved his hand in the air in an effort to get them to settle down a bit. "Look, I completely understand. And you should know I'm all for your idea of a homeless shelter. I've contributed some funds of my own. But a politician like that is only going to create chaos for Sunny Cove."

"Why?" Sammy wanted to know. "I can see this as a boost to our local economy, even if you don't count the possibilities for the homeless. People from surrounding towns will want to come here to hear Montgomery speak. That means they'll buy gas here, they'll eat here, and they might even want to stay in the hotel."

Jones sighed. "Yes. And that's great, to a point. But that also means there will be quite a few new faces around here. People we don't know usually means trouble, is my experience."

"Don't be so closed-minded," Rob admonished. "We've got to have some new blood around here sometimes."

"And," Jones continued, ignoring him, "I've made it a policy never to trust people in politics. They tell you they're just running for office because they want to help people, but they always have some personal agenda."

Sammy cast him a stern look before turning to Rob and pasting a smile on her face. "Tell me when will he arrive?"

"Monday," Rob replied breathlessly. "We only have a few days to get this going."

"Monday?" she squeaked. "Wow. How are we going to make that work?"

"I've already called the Logan Hotel and reserved the biggest, nicest room."

Sammy shook her head. "Shouldn't we put him up in a nicer place, like maybe over in Oak Hills?" The Logan Hotel was a neat old place that'd been built over a hundred years ago. A two-story brick edifice, it was the only place to stay if you wanted to be right in Sunny Cove. Under new management about five years ago, it'd been cleaned up and some of the historical elements added back in while still offering cable television and air conditioning. That was all fine, but it probably wasn't the kind of place a famous actor would expect.

"No, I already thought about that. My friend said Mr. Montgomery wants to get out and really see what's going on in small towns across the state, and he doesn't need anyone to think he's some sort of snob. The Logan Hotel will be perfect."

"Okay, so what else?" Sammy was still making a point not to look at Sheriff Jones, who was glaring at each of them in turn.

"We need to come up with some venues where he can do his speeches. They need to be big enough to house a crowd, but we don't have a lot of places like that around here." He ran a hand through his hair, giving evidence as to how it'd gotten that way in the first place.

Sammy chewed her lip. "What about the lobby of the hotel itself? It's nice and open, and it wouldn't take a lot of effort to rig up a stage at one end. There's plenty of parking across the street, and we might even get some extra guests at the hotel if they know they can have everything they need right at one location."

Rob snapped his fingers. "It's perfect! I'll call the hotel back and arrange it. I doubt they'd have a problem with it, and I'll happily pay whatever fee they require. Now, um, I hate to ask you this, but…"

"What is it?" Sammy urged.

"I know I can arrange for some refreshments with the hotel, but they'll just buy cheap sugar cookies in bulk and serve equally cheap coffee. I really want to impress Mr. Montgomery, and I thought maybe if you were able to put out some of your special treats…"

Sammy laughed as she slapped him playfully on the arm. "You don't even have to ask! Of course I will. I'm just as invested in this as you are."

"Great! Make it something really easy to serve, so we don't have to worry too much about staffing. Maybe cupcakes or cookies. We'll have to make sure we've got some security going, too. Sheriff, do you think your boys can work some overtime?" Rob turned to the stool next to him, but it was empty. "Where did he go?"

2
MOVIE NIGHT

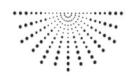

Sammy looked up from her notebook when the knock sounded at her front door. She dropped her pen and trotted into the living room, whipping the door open to admit Chelsea. "I'm so glad you're here to study with me!"

"Study? Don't put it that way, or I'm going back home!" Chelsea stepped inside, unwrapping a cashmere scarf from around her neck and hanging it on a hook by the door.

"Okay, okay," Sammy relented, closing the door against the elements. Sunny Cove had gotten past it's worst cold spell at the very beginning of the year, but it was still too frigid to risk letting all the heat out. "How about research? Is that better?"

"You could just call it what it is and say it's an excuse to watch old movies," Chelsea said with a grin. "I even brought some microwaveable popcorn, just in case you didn't have any. Extra butter, of course." She held out the tote bag she'd brought.

"That'll be a perfect pairing with the soda I have in the fridge and the pizza I have on the way!" Sammy clapped her hands, truly excited for a girls' night in. True, it was for a certain purpose, and one that hopefully would help her community out in the long run, but that didn't mean she couldn't have a little bit of fun on the way.

"So, tell me a little bit about this Montgomery guy," Chelsea said as she followed Sammy to the kitchen.

Sammy put a bag of popcorn in the microwave before turning to her friend. "You've seriously never heard of Stephen Montgomery before?"

Her friend shook her head. "Pretty sure I haven't! I've never been one for watching older movies, though."

"I'm sure you'll recognize him as soon as you see his face. And I guess I can't say too much. We wouldn't be having this movie night if I didn't feel like I needed to brush up on his life before he comes to town. I just really don't want to introduce myself without knowing more about him."

"I can understand that. I wonder if his movies have much to do with his political career. I can't imagine going from stage and screen to being a mayor." Chelsea picked up the stack of DVD's Sammy had rented from the video store and began flipping through them.

"Looks like he might've played some political roles in the past, but it's not like he's the first actor to get into government. There have been plenty of others." Sammy had already looked up other famous actors who'd served as governors and mayors or held congressional seats. "It makes sense, in a way, because they already have some popularity they can build on. If I wanted to run for governor, nobody would have a clue who I am."

"Maybe not, but they would if you were running for an office here in Sunny Cove. I bet you could at least get on the city council," Chelsea commented, flipping over one of the DVD cases and looking at the back.

"No, thanks!" Sammy got out a couple of big plastic bowls to use for popcorn and got the sodas out of the fridge.

"Why not? You'd be great at it, and you tend to get involved in community issues anyway. I mean, otherwise you'd never be so enthusiastic about this guy coming to town," Chelsea argued.

She had to admit that much was true, but it still wasn't enough to get Sammy interested in anything quite like that. "Yes, I do get involved, but I think I prefer it as a voluntary thing I do every now and then instead of my job. You hear of people who take their hobby they love and try to turn it into a profession, and that's when they start to lose interest in it. I don't want to do that with my community work. I mean, it sounds great to just spend all day thinking of ways to help the people of Sunny Cove, but I wouldn't want to start resenting the work because I felt obligated to it."

"I guess that makes sense." The two women went back into the living room just as the pizza showed up, and then they turned their conversation away from Sammy's potential councilwoman to Stephen Montgomery's acting career as they started one of his movies.

"It's been a while since I watched an old movie. It's so funny to think how different they are from current movies. It's kind of nice." Sammy found herself getting immersed in a world of no cell phones or flat screen TV's, when things seemed a little bit simpler and more straightforward. Sure, there was still plenty of drama between the hero (played by Montgomery, of course) and the heroine, but it all resolved itself in the end. She liked those happy endings.

"This is great," Chelsea said as she switched out the DVD's, "but have you looked up his biography online or anything?"

Sammy had to laugh at herself. She'd gotten so lost in the world of fifty years ago that she hadn't even thought about it. She quickly pulled out her laptop. "Let's see if his campaign manager has covered all the bases."

She skipped past the community-built pages and went directly to his official site, wanting the most accurate information. "It says here that he grew up in a small town in Indiana on the edge of a farm, and his family was literally dirt poor. He got his big break when he happened to travel to California with a friend of his who was starting college out there."

"Oh, look at this!" Chelsea was looking up information on her phone as well. "Further down the page it details his life in his early twenties when he was homeless. I guess this would've been before he made it big. He was riding the rails, digging his meals out of dumpsters, and begging for money in the streets."

"No way! Let me see!"

Chelsea showed her what she'd found, which included an old black-and-white photo of Stephen Montgomery looking rather dirty and ragged as he slept in a cardboard box.

"It all makes perfect sense now," Sammy mused. "That's why he's focusing so much on the issue of homelessness for his campaign. He's been there before, and he knows what these people are feeling." Sammy felt a thrill shoot through her chest. "This is so exciting! We've got someone who's not just famous, but who really gets it. I can't wait to hear him speak!"

"Sounds like you'll have to join his fan club." Chelsea pointed to the tab on the webpage Sammy had pulled up.

"You know, I think I just might," Sammy replied with a grin.

"Oh, check this out." Chelsea showed Sammy another picture, this one of Stephen Montgomery in a fine suit standing among a bunch of ragged and barefoot people on a sidewalk. Some of them were even barefoot. "'The grand opening of the Soup Saloon, where local homeless people can come for a free meal. Jobs are also offered to those who want to enter their program, all sponsored by Mayor Stephen Montgomery,' Sammy read. "Wow, looks like he really knows how to get the ball rolling."

"Oh, yeah. I'm just skimming here, but I'm seeing all sorts of projects that he's had his fingers in. He's helped rebuild the local parks, volunteered at the humane society, read books to children at the library, and it looks like he hosts a clothing and food drive for the homeless every year. We need this guy in our town!"

"And he will be, in just a couple of days." Sammy felt a small ripple of nervousness at meeting the bigshot. "It's not every day we have a Hollywood actor come through Sunny Cove. I hope Rob and I do a good enough job of setting everything up for him." Even as she spoke about it, her fingers itched to get baking so there would be plenty of treats for the receptions.

"You'll be fine," Chelsea assured her. "First of all, the two of you truly care and are excited about this. That in itself will go a long way toward this being a success. The other important thing to remember is that he might have had his time on the silver screen, but Mr. Montgomery is still just a human. And if he's been traveling around the state and working with homeless people, he can't be too much of a snob."

"I guess that's true," Sammy replied as she flipped through some of the photos on the site once again. "You know, it's funny that it's always actors or politicians—or in this case, both—who have the time to really tackle the big issues. Average working people don't have the time to lobby Congress or stage protests or fundraise full time."

"Maybe that's true, but I don't think he did all of this by himself," Chelsea pointed out. "There had to be enough people in his community who cared, too, or he wouldn't get elected."

"True enough." Sammy tried to turn her thoughts away from her worries about getting everything ready for the visiting politician and focus on the next movie. It was hard to believe that the man she was watching on the screen might soon be their governor, even though she knew he wasn't the first actor to go into politics. Every now and then, her stomach jerked with nervous excitement, and she hoped this visit would truly be as significant for Sunny Cove as she thought it could be.

3

NEW IN TOWN

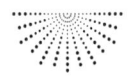

Sammy rubbed the insides of her knees together in a nervous dance as she waited in the lobby of the Logan Hotel. She'd purchased her outfit specifically for the occasion once she realized she didn't own much that was on the more formal side. The charcoal gray skirt suit had been an easy choice when she'd run out of the house in between baking cookies and cupcakes and a few special turnovers, and with Chelsea's help she'd managed to get a few other outfits to wear during the mayor's visit as well.

Even though she knew everything was as ready as it could possibly be, Sammy was convinced they were forgetting something. "We did give them the right address to the hotel, didn't we?" she asked Rob.

He was standing beside her, looking incredibly cool considering the circumstances. He was always wearing a suit, and this didn't seem like anything more than a typical day in court for him. "Of course I did."

"And they have his room ready to go? I wouldn't want there to be any delays in allowing him to get settled once he gets here. He might be tired from his time on the road." Stephen Montgomery might have ridden the rails as a hobo back in his day, but he was in his seventies now.

He turned and gave her a pointed look. "It's only a two-hour drive. I thought I was the one who was going to be a mess, Sammy. Why are you so worried?"

"I just want everything to be perfect," she explained. "This is our only chance at getting this kind of attention for the shelter we want to build. It might be nothing more than a stop on the campaign trail to him or to anyone else, but it's a lot more than that to me." She distinctly felt that the future of the local homeless community was resting squarely on her shoulders.

"Don't be so hard on yourself," he admonished. "Everything is going to be just fine. The hotel manager allowed me to go into the suite Montgomery will be using and inspect it myself, just to be sure. Sheriff Jones is waiting out on the edge of town to escort the limousine down Main Street, and Sunny Cove has put on its typical fanfare when there's anything exciting going on. I've seen flags hanging out in front of businesses, windows painted with welcome messages, and even the street sweepers have come through. This is truly Sunny Cove at its best."

Sammy straightened her suit jacket. "I sure hope you're right."

The faint sound of sirens came through the windows at the front of the hotel, and Sammy's heart soared and fell in time with the noise.

"That's them," Rob announced. "Let's greet them outside."

"Sounds good," she replied breathlessly.

The February air was chilly in her lungs, but Sammy hardly noticed it. She was actually much more grateful to get out of the cozy warmth of the hotel lobby that was starting to become stifling. She flapped her elbows to circulate the chill under her arms.

The spectacle down the street was something she'd never seen in Sunny Cove. First in the impromptu parade was a squad car driven by Sheriff Jones himself with full lights and sirens going. A long dark limousine followed along behind him. Several more police cars flanked the rear. That was all exciting enough, but it was all according to plan. What Sammy hadn't expected was the thick crowds that clogged the sidewalks on either side of Main Street. Folks had come out in their winter coats, with thick scarves wrapped around their faces and wool hats pulled down firmly over their ears, just to wave at the car. They held up their children and babies in order to see better, and at least a few of them were throwing homemade confetti.

Sheriff Jones wouldn't appreciate that, but at the moment he was too occupied with his job as official escort to worry about it. As he pulled up to the curb in front of the hotel, pulling forward enough to leave room for the limousine right in front of the doors, Sammy noticed the grim look on his face. He didn't look at her, keeping his gaze straight ahead.

The length of Montgomery's limo seemed endless as it glided up to the curb, miles and miles of gleaming black sliding by. Sammy could see her reflection, distorted and nervous, in that smooth finish. She did her best to rearrange her face and look professional and happy.

A short man with a balding head leaped out of the back of the limo. He snapped upright as he held the door open. There was no mistaking Stephen Montgomery when he stepped out of the car. He was incredibly tall, even taller than he looked in his movies. His face had aged considerably since those younger days, but he still carried a sparkle in his pale blue eyes. He'd lost his thick, dark hair, which had been replaced with wisps of gray. His distinctive, wide mouth stretched into a smile as he turned to those waiting for him on the sidewalk and held out his hand. "I'm Stephen Montgomery. Thank you so much for hosting me here in your lovely little town."

Rob shook his hand. "It's very nice to meet you, Mr. Montgomery. I'm Rob Hewitt, and this is Samantha Baker."

"Please, call me Stephen." He shook Sammy's hand next.

He was well past his time as a Hollywood bigshot, but Sammy was still starstruck. She had to stop herself from curtsying, and she knew she'd never be able to address him by his first name. "Your room is all ready to go for you. We'd be happy to walk you up."

"And if you have a moment once you get your luggage dropped off and get cleaned up from the road, we'd like to talk to you about your schedule while you're here in town." Rob held open the front door of the hotel.

"Not a problem at all," the mayor replied amicably as he stepped inside and took in the pale yellows and pinks of the Logan Hotel before turning back to the short man who bustled in behind him. "This is Rudy Rush, my campaign manager."

Rudy shook each of their hands, his palms sweaty. Sammy noticed a few beads of sweat stood out on his forehead despite the chilly weather and realized she wasn't the only one who was a little nervous. "Thank you so much for having us. This is quite a reception, I must say. Couldn't have put it together better myself."

"If you mean the crowd on the street, that wasn't our doing," Rob pointed out. "All we did was make sure everyone knew you were coming to Sunny Cove. I think the citizens are genuinely excited to hear what you have to say."

They were just crossing the patterned carpet to the old elevator when Tim came running to intercept their path, a roll of yellow caution tape fluttering from his hand. He worked for the Logan Hotel, serving in almost every position available depending on how short-staffed they were for the day. "I'm sorry," he panted, his cheeks flushing with embarrassing. "The elevator is having some technical difficulties, and I'm afraid you'll have to take the stairs."

Sammy felt her own cheeks heat up. They had and important man in their town, one who would possibly be the governor in a few months, and they didn't even have a working elevator. "I'm so sorry, Mr. Montgomery. I hate to make you hike up all those stairs, since your suite is on the third floor…" She trailed off, looking to Rob for some assistance, hoping he got her mental messages about putting him up in a different hotel in the next town.

But Mr. Montgomery waved his hand and turned on his heel toward the curving staircase at the other end of the lobby. "Nonsense! I could use a little exercise, couldn't I?"

Maybe he could, but Sammy was cringing by the time they reached the top floor. She was used to working in good sneakers with an anti-stress mat under her all day, not climbing wooden stairs in heels. She was suddenly grateful for how casual the dress code was at Just Like Grandma's.

"Here's your suite," Rob announced, opening the door and handing the keys to Rudy. "It's said that President Ronald Reagan stayed in this very room while on his campaign route. I've arranged a room next door for Mr. Rush."

Tim and a bellboy rushed in from the hallway just then. They panted as they lugged the suitcases behind them. "Um, I'm afraid there's going to be a small problem with that."

Now even Rob was beginning to get flustered. "And what would that be?" He asked the question calmly, but Sammy could see the fire in his eyes and see how tense his shoulders were becoming under his suit jacket.

"Um, well, there's been a bit of a leak," Tim tried to explain. "You know how all this old plumbing is. It's part of the, um, *charm* of running such a historic building."

"Charm, indeed," Sammy muttered under her breath. To Tim, she said more loudly, "Then can we please arrange a different room for Mr. Rush?"

"Ah, oh." Tim puffed out his cheeks and let the air escape through pursed lips. "I would love to do that, but all the other rooms are booked in anticipation of Mr. Montgomery's visit. The best I could do is to arrange for a room at a bed-and-breakfast on the outskirts of town. Well, maybe. If they're not completely booked. I could call the Super 8 over in Oak Hills…"

"Don't go to such a fuss," Mr. Montgomery intoned smoothly. "There's plenty of room in here for both of us, and Rudy and I are used to traveling together on the road. Isn't that right, Rudy?"

"Of course, sir. Absolutely, sir. That will work a little better for security purposes, as well." He crossed the room to peer through the windows, frowning.

"Security?" Sammy questioned.

"Absolutely!" Rudy turned back toward the little crowd in the hotel room. "A prominent man like Mr. Montgomery must be protected at all times."

Rob stepped forward. "I can assure you, Sunny Cove is a very safe little town. Everyone knows everyone else here, and—"

But Mr. Rush was holding up a finger. "That's a very common mistake that many people make. People assume that just because they're not in a big city that they're safe. But things can happen anywhere." He strode to the door and checked the functionality of the lock. "Is this a solid wood door?"

Mr. Montgomery cleared his throat pointedly. "I'm sorry. As usual my campaign manager is thinking a little bit too much. That's exactly why I hired him, though. He and I used to work on the set together all the time, and I knew he'd be the perfect partner. But we'll be just fine here in this room, and there's nothing further to worry about. Isn't that right, Rudy?"

The campaign manager looked slightly disappointed, but he nodded. "Yes, I suppose so."

"There, now. If you can just bring in a cot and put it right over there, we'll be right as rain." The mayor pointed to a space next to the dresser, where a potted plant could easily be moved out of the way.

"I'll do that, sir." Tim left the luggage by the door while he and his bellboy jogged out into the hall.

"Well, we'll leave you to it," Rob said, urging Sammy toward the exit as well. "If you don't mind, we'll just hang out at the end of the hall until you're ready for us. Save us a trip up and down the stairs." He gave a nervous laugh.

"Of course, of course! We won't be long, I promise." The actor closed the door behind them.

Sammy felt as though her heels were clicking far too loudly as they headed down the hardwood floor of the hallway, and when they reached the window seat at the end of the hall she gladly sat down and took them off. "I don't think that could've gone any worse."

Rob sighed as he settled down next to her. "I'd love to argue with you. I really would, but I don't think I can. The only saving grace is that Mr. Montgomery doesn't seem too frazzled by any of it."

"I guess he can't be too picky, considering his earlier years." She took a few minutes to quietly explain what she'd learned about the actor's time spent sleeping on the streets.

Her companion raised a blonde eyebrow. "I didn't realize that. Makes sense, though."

"I thought so, too. I just hope the rest of his visit goes more smoothly." She shouldn't have, but she allowed her mind to wander over everything else that could possibly go wrong. What if the stage gave way while Mr. Montgomery gave his speech? What if a freak snowstorm came along and kept him trapped in Sunny Cove? What if something was wrong with one of the cookies she made, or the candidate was on a strict no-sugar diet?

"Stop it."

"Stop what?" She looked at Rob, astonished.

"I know that look on your face. You're getting too worried about this, and that's not going to help things at all. We've got everything under control—at least, everything we *can* have under control. It's not our fault the elevator broke or that Rudy's room has leaky pipes. And maybe that's just God's way of getting all the 'bad stuff' out of the way so that everything else can go smoothly."

Sammy had to admire his positive attitude, even if she didn't exactly share it. "I do have all the refreshments ready to go for tomorrow. I thought it might be a nice idea to invite Mr. Montgomery to Just Like Grandma's for dinner tonight, so he can have a good meal on his first night here. I've heard the room service here leaves something to be desired."

"There, see? Everything is fine."

"Maybe so, but I don't think I can sit still any longer." Sammy launched to her feet, fueled by nervous energy. "I think I'll go downstairs and see if Tim needs any help finding a cot. With our current luck, he'll have discovered that the supply closet has been raided by aliens or something." Still in her stocking feet, she padded toward the staircase on the other end of the hallway.

But as she passed Mr. Montgomery's room, she could hear raised voices from inside. Sammy knew it was wrong, but she slowed down to hear as much as possible.

"—believe this place?" Mr. Montgomery questioned. "I hired you because I knew you could help me with the governor's seat, but I didn't know it involved mucking through such Podunk little backwaters like this. I don't even think there's cable!"

Rudy mumbled something unintelligible through the thick door.

"And a broken elevator?" the candidate continued. "If they're looking for a claim to fame, it'll be that I died of a heart attack on the stairs!"

The voices were getting closer to the door, and Sammy turned to head back the way she'd come.

"What's wrong?" Rob asked.

But she just shook her head, as Rudy was opening the door to the room. He'd pasted a smile on his face as he gestured for them to come back inside. "Let's discuss that schedule, shall we?"

4
UNEXPECTED CHAOS

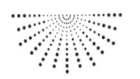

The smile on Sammy's face was a genuine one as she stood just to the side of the stage they'd erected at one end of the lobby and watched Mr. Montgomery give his speech to a packed crowd. The chairs that had been arranged were quickly filled and then the standing room taken up as the citizens of Sunny Cove and surrounding areas showed up. She knew the refreshments over on the side of the room would be well-received, and things were finally going smoothly. The only hiccup had been when Tim declared the room as full as possible without becoming a fire hazard, and she and Rob had engaged Sheriff Jones' help in controlling the crowd. They'd been somewhat mollified by the knowledge that there would be another speaking engagement held in two days, but the disallowed guests could still be seen milling about on the sidewalks just outside the large front windows of the Logan Hotel.

"In conclusion, I ask you to remember your fellow man," Mr. Montgomery pleaded from the podium. "We are all brothers and sisters in God's eyes, and we should be looking out for each other. Sometimes, we need a hand up, and sometimes we're in the position to give that hand. Even in small communities, there are those who just need a small step to get themselves going in the right direction. If I were to be elected governor, I would make it my priority to ensure every citizen in this state has a warm bed at night and food in their bellies. Thank you."

Sammy clapped heartily along with the crowd, feeling enthused all over again to help the homeless community in Sunny Cove. She hoped everyone else in attendance was feeling the same way, and she had such high hopes for what might happen if Mr. Montgomery were to be elected.

But that elation was quickly dashed as Sheriff Jones appeared at her elbow. His face was hard as he pulled her close. "You need to get Mr. Montgomery up to his room, quickly. A protest has just started outside."

"What?" She jerked her head to the side to see through the window. Her first thought had been that people were rebelling because they weren't allowed in, but that didn't seem to be the case. Behind the faces plastered to the window with interest was a different group, carrying signs and chanting. "Why?"

"Seems not everyone agrees with his platform," Sheriff Jones growled. "I've got all my men out in the streets. I need you and Rob to watch Mr. Montgomery and make sure he's safe."

"Okay. We'll do it." She quickly passed the information on to Rob and Mr. Rush as Sheriff Jones headed back outside. The foursome skipped the question-and-answer session as well as the refreshments as they made their way to the stairs and up to the presidential suite.

"I really don't think this is necessary," Mr. Montgomery protested. "I don't want to be the kind of person who runs away from a little bit of conflict."

"That might be fine, if we knew exactly why they were protesting," Sammy pointed out. "The safest thing to do for now is to get out of the way and let the sheriff's department do their job. Everyone will have another chance to see you on Wednesday." She couldn't help but think of the protests that had started just a few months ago when she'd first begun petitioning on behalf of those living on the streets. She'd been astonished that anyone would feel so vehemently about the issue, but some folks were afraid that being kind to the homeless would attract the wrong types of people to Sunny Cove. She'd thought all of that had been resolved, but she wouldn't really know until she got a report from Sheriff Jones on the matter.

"If you say so," Mr. Montgomery relented.

Rudy's hands shook as he tried to fit the key into the lock. "You see, this is exactly what I was worried about when it comes to security. Politicians and actors alike draw large crowds, and there's no telling who they might consist of. It takes all kinds to run a village, but only certain kinds to ruin an event like this."

Sammy was surprised at his cynical outlook. "I assure you, this isn't how things normally go in Sunny Cove."

Rudy's hands shook even harder as the key missed the lock entirely. "That's what everyone thinks, Miss Baker. Not in my town. Not around here. That only happens in the city. Let me assure *you*, it happens everywhere."

"Let me help you with that." Rob stepped forward and took the key from the campaign manager, who clearly wasn't going to get the door open anytime that day. He slipped it in the lock and swung the door open, gesturing for the two out-of-towners to precede him. "We should look on the bright side. I wouldn't mind taking advantage of this time and asking your opinion on our plans for the homeless shelter here in Sunny Cove, Mr. Montgomery."

But as they all entered the room, any future plans were forced to wait. A chilly wind blasted through the room, coming in through an open window. No, not open, Sammy quickly realized. Broken. The brick that had done the job was lying on the hardwood floor, a piece of paper rubber banded around it.

Sammy put a hand to her mouth. "Oh!"

But Rudy sighed and strode forward to pick up the offending object.

"Don't touch that!" Rob warned. "You might ruin any fingerprints. We need to let the police handle this."

But Rudy scooped up the brick and ripped off the note. "Not likely. A porous surface like that isn't going to hold fingerprints very well, and a small town like this probably doesn't have the sort of crime scene investigation equipment it would require. Trust me. I've been through this before."

"You have?" Sammy didn't like the sound of that.

"Oh, yes," replied Mr. Montgomery, who'd folded his tall frame into an upholstered chair on the opposite side of the room from the windows. "I'm afraid this isn't the first time we've found a brick through the window."

"It's happened in several of the other towns we've toured," Rudy explained. "I don't know what someone's problem is, but it's always something similar." He held up the note, which read, "I know."

"I know?" Sammy read out loud. "Know what?"

"Beats me," Montgomery said with a sigh. "Can we get someone up here to clean this up and board up the window. I'm starting to feel a little tired."

"Of course. Give me just a moment." Sammy beat Rob to the door, grateful she'd chosen more sensible shoes for the day now that she knew she'd be going up and down the stairs. She gripped the carved banister, worn smooth by decades of use, and thundered down to the lobby. She found Tim behind the front desk, looking frazzled at the pure amount of people still in attendance and wondering when Mr. Montgomery had gone.

"You're kidding!" he said with wide eyes when Sammy filled him in on the broken glass and the nasty note. "I don't want to touch any of it until Sheriff Jones says it's all right."

"I agree, but you might want to get your hands on some plywood, considering we don't have any other place to put Mr. Montgomery for the night. I'll find the sheriff." Sammy elbowed her way through the crowd, her heart thundering loudly in her ears despite the noise of the throng around her. Any one of them could've been the culprit, even those who'd seemed enraptured by the mayor's speech. Sammy had no way of knowing how long ago the brick had been thrown. She turned her attention to the protestors being scattered in the street, but they were on the wrong side of the building. The windows to the presidential suite were on the back of the building, facing the park.

She nearly ran into Sheriff Jones as he came back in the front door of the hotel, his cheeks pink from the cold. "What are you doing here?" he demanded. "You're supposed to be with Mr. Montgomery."

"That's just the thing. We've had a bit of an incident."

He didn't need to hear any more before he rushed behind her back up the stairs to see for himself.

"I've got Tim getting ready with a hammer and nails, but I knew you'd want to see it first." She stepped aside as she walked into the hotel room, giving Sheriff Jones a wide berth to investigate the scene.

Rudy turned back into his normal nervous self as soon as he saw a man in uniform. "This is just the sort of thing I was concerned about," he lectured, shaking the note at the sheriff, who was easily a head taller than he was. "Things happen on the campaign trail, but we need to do everything in our power to prevent it. I don't know what your officers were doing tonight, Jones. Maybe they were too busy enjoying the cookies or something."

Sammy felt offended at the suggestion, but Jones was staying calm and collected. "I've had an awful lot to deal with during this visit," he said quietly. "But I can assure you my best detective is on the case."

As Rudy continued to prattle on about how unsafe Sunny Cove was, Sheriff Jones swung his gaze pointedly to Sammy and winked.

5

THE GRAND TOUR

"I can't tell you how sorry I am about yesterday," Rob said, taking a sip of coffee. The four of them—Rob, Sammy, Mr. Montgomery, and Rudy Rush—had assembled in the breakfast room of the Logan Hotel the next morning. The place held an entirely different atmosphere than it had the day before. The crowd had dispersed once the cookies and cupcakes had been consumed, and Tim and his staff had returned the place to its normal state of classic elegance.

Mr. Montgomery looked tired, but he waved a dismissive hand. "You shouldn't worry about it, nor should you take the blame. As Rudy said, these things happen. There's obviously someone who is not interested in seeing me as governor. You know, I expected some pretty difficult pushback, being that I'm not a lifelong politician, but I never thought people would stoop so low until we set out on this tour."

"Even so, I'd really like to take you out on a tour of Sunny Cove. I know you'll have a couple of other events while you're here, but I'd love for you to get a real taste of what this town is about. It'll be even prettier in the summer, of course, but I think you'll get the idea." Rob beamed at the mayor.

But Mr. Montgomery shook his head. "I don't want to drag the two of you out in the cold."

"We don't mind a bit," Sammy chimed in. She'd spent half the previous night awake, wondering what on earth they were going to do to prevent any more disasters from happening while Mr. Montgomery was around. But the truth remained that she had no way of preventing them when she couldn't predict what those disasters would be. Sheriff Jones had agreed to post a man outside the actor's hotel door throughout the night, but there was little else they could do. "And I know that word about you has really spread. Our own homeless community wouldn't mind getting the chance to meet you and know they have someone advocating for them besides us locals."

"Well, we'll have to see if we can fit it into the schedule. Rudy?"

The campaign manager flipped through the notepad attached to the clipboard he'd been carrying around. "Well, I have a few things I need to take care of today. But I could stay here at the hotel and make some calls, and you could go."

"Are you sure?"

Rudy checked a few more pages. "Yes. Yes, I'm sure."

"All right, then. I'll get my coat."

Rob volunteered to drive, and Sammy climbed in the back seat. She felt excited and important being able to give such a prominent person a look around Sunny Cove. The events of the previous evening had been terrible, but the sun was shining brightly and she was determined to put it behind her. At least, mostly.

"Most of the buildings you see here in the downtown area have some sort of historical significance," Rob offered as he cruised down the main road. "Sunny Cove has been around for almost two hundred years. Of course, not all the buildings are original. There was a rather unexpected tornado that came through about a hundred years ago and took out quite a bit of the town. Of course, everyone rallied and rebuilt, confident that we had many more years ahead of us."

Mr. Montgomery bobbed his head as he glanced all around him at the various buildings. Rob drove him past the post office and the courthouse, showed him the oldest home in Sunny Cove, and even pointed out numerous small businesses.

"Seems like you folks have a lot of town pride," Mr. Montgomery commented. "That's an important thing. So many are eager to pick up and move to a bigger city, because they think that's where all the excitement is. Let me tell you, I've been in some very big cities. Sure, there are a lot of bright lights and plenty of entertainment, but these little out-of-the-way places are the heart of America."

"I completely agree," Rob replied. "Unfortunately, as you probably know, we have many of the same problems that the bigger cities do. They're just ignored because they're on a smaller scale. I'd like to take you around to see where those who are a little less fortunate congregate on a regular basis." He turned and headed toward the grocery store.

"I don't want to create any kind of fuss," Mr. Montgomery hesitated. "I know I've already stirred up a bit of trouble here. Accidentally, of course."

"It's no fuss or trouble," Sammy assured from the back seat. "You see, Rob and I have been really trying to change things for these people. Some of them are from right here in Sunny Cove, while others have traveled in from goodness-knows-where. But we believe there needs to be a better place for them than back alleys and parking lots. We've worked with business and churches to serve as warming shelters, and we've hosted several dinners, but that doesn't help them in the long term."

Now Mr. Montgomery was on a soapbox he was comfortable with. "You're right, Miss Baker. They need more than just a hot meal. And they even need more than jobs. They need purpose and motivation. Otherwise, what's the point?"

Rob pulled around the grocery store to the back. Cliff and Judy were there, adding fuel to a barrel of burning trash. They waved and smiled when they recognized Rob and Sammy, but they peered suspiciously at the newcomer. Carter and Cooper were there with them, as well as several others whom Sammy recognized.

"Hey, guys. This is Stephen Montgomery," Rob began when he got out of the car. "He's currently running for governor, and the homeless issue is one that he's really concentrating on. I thought I'd take the chance to introduce you guys."

"Nice to meet you!" Cliff enthused, sticking out one grubby hand and offering a yellowed smile. "This is my wife, Judy. These fellas here are Carter and Cooper. The one in the blue hat is Troy. And this here is—Buckets? Where are ya?"

He looked around for a minute until a scruffy man poked his head out from behind the dumpster. His cloud of curly gray hair framed a dirty face with a pug nose and a thick mustache. He took one glance at the politician and dove back into his hiding spot.

"You'll have to forgive him. He can be a bit shy sometimes. PTSD, you know," Cliff explained. "It's awful nice to meet you. There aren't many people who sympathize with us. They just think we're a bunch of bums who don't want to work. But that's not the case at all."

"Yes. Nice to meet you as well." Stephen shook the man's hand but was careful not to touch himself with that hand afterwards. "I know Mr. Hewitt and

Miss Baker have been working very hard on your behalf, and it's my hope that I can help them do that."

"My schedule is free for consultation," Cliff joked, and his wife and the brothers laughed along with him. "We've got a lot of ideas, and we want to keep others off the streets just as much as we'd like to get off them ourselves."

"I'm sure you do. I think that might have to wait for another time, though." Mr. Montgomery ducked against the bitter wind that had kicked up. "I'm not sure my old bones can take the chill. I think I need to be getting back."

"Of course. We can take you back right away. We'll see you guys." Rob escorted the mayor back to the car.

Sammy followed along behind them, feeling terrible about getting this man out of the weather without being able to do the same for all of them. True, Mr. Montgomery was an older man, and he wasn't acclimated to spending extended amounts of time outside. But it just seemed so unfair for them to retreat to the warmth of the hotel and then their respective homes when Cliff and Judy had no place to go.

Back in the car, she was still mulling over this imbalance when Stephen turned around to address her. "Do you have any hand sanitizer? There's no telling what they might have on their hands."

6

PREPARING FOR THE WORST

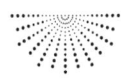

Sammy boxed up the last of the cookies and ran them out to the back of her Toyota, where they joined several other identical boxes, packages of cups, and jugs of tea and lemonade. She closed it up long enough to run back inside and wipe down all the counters from the mess she'd made with her baking and then touch up her hair before it was time to go.

She frowned into the mirror, thinking about what Chelsea had said. Could she be a city councilwoman? Did she really have what it took to not only care about the issues but to do something about them? She wasn't even sure she looked professional enough to be tagging along behind Mr. Montgomery, if she was honest with herself. Her curly blonde hair had gotten a little frizzy, and the freckles across her cheekbones that refused to go away even in the winter were showing through her makeup. Sammy captured her curls and twisted them up, pinning them into a chignon that looked a little more sleek and sophisticated. She dabbed on some extra foundation and powder, and even added a little more eyeliner. Mostly satisfied, she headed to Sunny Cove Services.

This speaking engagement was supposed to be the second and final one on Mr. Montgomery's tour of Sunny Cove, but after the massive crowd that'd turned out for his speech at the hotel Rob assured him he would arrange at least one more. He wanted everyone to get a chance to hear what the politician had to say, and there just weren't many venues in town that were big enough to make that happen.

Sammy arrived at Sunny Cove Services early, wanting plenty of time to set up the refreshments before she had to deal with anything else that went wrong. She was starting to give up hope of things going smoothly, since that just didn't seem to be in the cards.

"Hi, Sammy!" Austin darted forward to get the door for her as she tried to balance too many boxes of cookies on her way in. "I came to help!"

"You did? That was very nice of you. And I think I could definitely use some help." Sammy set her load down on a nearby table and gave Austin a hug. He was mentally disabled and had experienced some trouble in the past, but Sammy had helped him turn his life around when she and Rob had established Sunny Cove Services. It was a place for those like Austin to gain meaningful employment while learning real-work skills. They built boxes, shredded paper, and stuffed envelopes. When they weren't working, Sammy and others in the community taught them how to cook, sew, and clean. It was incredibly rewarding to know she'd helped with this, but it was also disheartening to know she hadn't been able to do the same for the homeless. "How's Uncle Mitch?"

"Good. He's says he's tired of this darn weather. It hurts his hands."

Sammy looked sympathetically into his wide green eyes under his curtain of wild black hair. "I'm sure it does. Are you helping him around the house?"

"Oh, yes! He showed me how to change the filter in the furnace. Did you know the ancient Romans put furnaces in their homes almost three thousand years ago?" His eyes grew even wider at reciting his knowledge. Austin had a penchant for watching documentaries and reading books just to memorize all the little facts.

"I didn't know that, but now I do. Thank you for sharing with me. Will you help me get the rest of the stuff out of my car?"

He clapped his hands. "Yes!"

Sammy loved his enthusiasm, and she smiled as they each loaded their arms down. "What else have you been up to, besides helping Uncle Mitch with the furnace?"

"We had a pizza party the other day. Miss Faye said we'd been doing a really good job, and I love pepperoni pizza. But then there was that man." Austin opened the door and let her go through first.

The jugs were heavy, so she set them down before turning back to him with concern. "What man?"

Austin's normally happy face puckered into a sour one. "I don't know. I didn't know him, and he was hanging out behind the building."

"Hmm." Sammy had to wonder if this was one of the homeless folks. Buckets, who'd hidden from Stephen Montgomery the previous day, hadn't been in town very long. If Austin had seen him, he might not've recognized him. "What did he look like?"

Austin rolled his eyes to the ceiling to think. "He had long hair and a big nose."

That didn't sound like Buckets or anyone else Sammy could think of offhand. "What was he doing behind the building?" She tried to keep her tone light so she wouldn't scare Austin.

"He was just standing out there, and when we came out to put the pizza boxes in the dumpster he left. Did you know October is national pizza month?"

"That's great." Sammy began arranging the tables and the goodies on top of them, trying not to worry too much about the stranger out by the dumpster. But it was difficult, given that someone had thrown that brick through Mr. Montgomery's hotel window. She also couldn't ignore what Sheriff Jones had said about the politician's visit bringing new people into town. Sammy had no question that Jones expected her to solve the mystery of the brick, but she didn't have a whole lot to go on just yet.

She was pulled away from her ponderings when she spotted Tim, coming in the front door with an armful of tablecloths. "My boss said you guys might need some extra supplies. I told him about the chaos of Mr. Montgomery's speech at the hotel, and he said we'll give you anything you need to help this go off without a hitch."

Sammy was incredibly grateful. "That's so nice of him! But he didn't have to do that. It wasn't the hotel's fault that things went a little crazy."

Tim shrugged. "Maybe not, but when things like that go down, the Logan Hotel risks losing some of its good reputation. He wanted to do anything possible to make it up to you. I'm at your service for the rest of the evening."

"But aren't you needed at the hotel?" Sammy pointed out. "You're always busy over there, and I know you're understaffed, especially since the place is booked."

"Yeah, but I don't dare go back there until the end of my shift," Tim grumbled as he helped Sammy move one of the tables into place. "I'm used to being a little busy, and I don't mind that. It's been great that so many people have come to town and decided to stay with us. But that Mr. Montgomery is more than a handful."

"Really? Was he upset about the window? I mean, he didn't seem like it when I was there, but it had to bother him." She'd had such high expectations for this visit and what it would do for their town. Now she was beginning to wonder if Sunny Cove, just like the Logan Hotel, might suffer for it.

"Oh, sure. The window. The plumbing. The mattress. The sheets. Even the hangers in the closet aren't good enough for him, because he says they put wrinkles in his suits. I showed him where the iron and the ironing board were, but that answer didn't sit very well with him."

Sammy bit her lip, thinking. "No, I suppose it didn't." Why was Mr. Montgomery so upset about the amenities at the Logan Hotel? He'd already berated Rudy over it, and now he was attacking Tim. But he always acted so unperturbable when she and Rob were around. "I'm really sorry about all this."

"Don't apologize. It's not your fault, and he's not the first person to be a little bit picky. You'd think when we advertise the hotel as 'historic' people would get the idea that it's not a brand-new building with all state-of-the-art accommodations. They should just be glad they have a roof over their heads, if you ask me."

"I couldn't agree with you more," Sammy said with a nod, thinking once again about Cliff, Judy, and the others out in the cold. "Say, do you have extra chairs you could bring over from the hotel? I'm not sure we'll have enough. I know people will pack in here like sardines, but I'm sure there'll be some old folks and disabled who need to sit down."

"Sure thing," Tim said with a nod.

"I'll help!" Austin volunteered.

Tim smiled at him and waved him out to the parking lot. "Let's go, buddy!"

7

HOPING FOR THE BEST

"Is there any way we can adjust these lights?" Rudy was at Sammy's elbow, squinting up at the lights on the ceiling of Sunny Cove Services. "They're far too harsh. They're going to make Stephen look much older than he is."

Sammy pressed her lips together as she glanced at Rob. This was just the latest iteration of dealing with Rudy. "I don't think there's much we can do about them."

The campaign manager wiped a slick of sweat off his brow. "That's not good. I knew I should've come here yesterday to check it out, and then maybe we could've brought in some different lights on stands."

"We didn't do anything to change the lighting at the hotel," Rob pointed out.

"And we didn't need to," Rudy said impatiently. "That old building is already dim, and it created a perfect atmosphere. But think about it, you two. Mr. Montgomery's presence is obviously creating a stir in this town. With all the chaos at the hotel, I fully expect this engagement to be even more in the public eye. I just wish I could control what kind of phones and cameras people record with. There's no telling how terrible their footage will be when they post it on social media."

"But it's not a movie. I don't see why it needs to be such a big production." Sammy wouldn't have made this argument if she hadn't spent the last hour with Rudy, talking about how the light would change as the sun went down, whether or not Mr. Montgomery's suit would go with the carpet, and if they needed to have more 'Montgomery for Governor' signs hanging on the stage. And then, of course, Rudy had insisted that the bunting along the bottom edge of the stage be steamed until it was free of any wrinkles.

This earned her another irritated sigh from the campaign manager. "And that's exactly why this is *my* job, and not yours. You don't understand. Every single thing that Stephen does will be in the public eye, and that means someone will be scrutinizing it.

It'll either reflect poorly on him or on me, and neither one is acceptable. I mean, I didn't work in the movie industry for two decades without learning a thing or two."

"Yes, Mr. Montgomery had mentioned that's how the two of you met. What, exactly, did you do?"

Rudy flapped a hand in the air as he darted forward to once again adjust the bunting. "You name it! I started out getting coffee on a sound stage for all the people who thought they were more important than me. I moved up to painting sets, and then as the times changed there were more options for special effects. I could've been a director if I'd stayed in the business."

"I see." And Sammy really did. At least Rudy's background gave some logic to his fuss over every aspect of this speaking engagement.

"The campaign trail is like one long, drawn-out movie," Rudy continued to explain as he straightened a row of chairs that Sammy had already fixed once. "But it's not as easy to control as it is when you're working in a studio. No, no. I have to deal with crowds of unpredictable people, terrible lighting, and venues that constantly change. We got lucky with that hotel, even if it is a bit of a dump."

"I'm sorry it's not to your satisfaction," Rob said stiffly.

"No, no. I'm sorry. I didn't mean it quite that way. And as I said, it worked very well for the speech. I just don't have high hopes for this place." He squinted up at the lights once again.

Sammy did the same, wondering what was so terrible about them. The grant money they'd received for establishing Sunny Cove Services went a long way toward their goal, but they'd still had to be careful with it. They'd opted for LED shop lights that were inexpensive and efficient, but they'd been geared more toward offering enough light to work by instead of making a seventy-year-old man look like he had a glowing, youthful complexion.

Tim showed up, panting a little. "People are starting to line up at the door. Should I let them in yet?"

Sammy looked to Rudy for the answer, not wanting to make the campaign manager any more anxious than he already was.

The little man bobbed his head. "Yes, that should be fine. Stephen is in the back room going over his speech. He's changing it up a little bit, so it won't be exactly the same as what he delivered at the hotel. That's another part of our little movie: the script can't ever stay the same, or people will stop watching." He bustled off to notify his boss that it was almost time to start.

"He's a bit uptight," Sammy commented to Rob.

"If you think that's bad, you should've seen him freak out when he asked me about the security of this place. I mean, I guess he doesn't understand that it's just a big room attached to an old theatre. There's nothing particularly secure about it, and it wasn't designed for this sort of function. You'd think he'd just be happy that we can arrange a room this size in a town so small. It probably didn't make him feel any better when I told him the police couldn't be here until after the event started."

"Well, it can't be helped when several of the officers are down with the flu and there are other emergencies around town." Sammy looked through the glass door, noting that none of the deputies had shown up just yet. "I have a feeling Sheriff Jones isn't going to talk to us again after this week."

Rob winked. "Don't worry. He'll talk to *you.*"

"What's that supposed to mean?"

But Rob unlocked the door and let the line of people file into the building, cutting off any further conversation.

Sammy did her best to help with crowd control, but Sunny Cove Services was still in complete chaos by the time Mr. Montgomery came out of the back room and stepped up onto the stage. As she found a chair for an elderly woman with a cane, she reflected on everything Rudy had said about the campaign being like a movie. He wasn't entirely wrong. Any politician would have to put on a bit of a show to get people to vote for him, just like actors had to do a good job with a film to encourage audiences to see it. In that sense, Rudy was probably the perfect person for a campaign manager. He'd just need to work a little more on being prepared to roll with the punches.

"I have to tell you folks what a lovely little town you have," Mr. Montgomery said, receiving loud cheers from the audience in response. "I'm not going to say it's perfect, because that would mean you didn't need anything. But I've seen for myself that there are people on the streets, people who need a warm bed and food in their bellies. They need a sense of purpose and a reason to change their lives. I understand that Mr. Hewitt and Miss Baker have been working hard to make that happen, but what you folks need to understand is that this isn't something they can do by themselves."

Sammy fought back the tears that threatened at the backs of her eyes as the crowd cheered once again.

"I highly encourage you to contribute what you can to this noble quest. Whether it be volunteering your time or donating a little extra cash, don't forget that you could just as easily end up in the same situation as those on the streets. You'd want someone to give you a hand up, and I say all humankind deserves that!" He clutched his fist in the air in front of him for emphasis.

It worked, since the crowd was starting to go wild.

But over the din, Sammy could hear something else. It was a chant, and it was coming from outside the building. She threaded her way through the crowd, not knowing what was going on but not liking the possibilities. When she finally reached the front door, she saw exactly what she didn't want to see. People were in the street in front of Sunny Cove Services, carrying signs and yelling. They were all directed at Mr. Montgomery, saying things like 'Politicians, not Actors' and 'The State is Not a Movie Set.' A simple protest might not have been so bad, but things looked like they were about to get ugly when some of those who were there in support of the candidate started yelling at the protestors.

"Thank you all so very much for listening to what I have to say," Mr. Montgomery was continuing. "And now I'd like to listen to what you have to say. We have a short amount of time for some questions."

But Sammy now knew that he really didn't. She wondered to herself how she'd been put on guard duty for a politician as she made her way back to the stage and informed Rudy of what was happening. "We need to get him out of here before things get worse."

"Agreed. I'll get on stage and address the crowd. You and Rob get him out back to the car."

"Right." Sammy found Rob as Rudy hopped up on the stage and whispered in the actor's ear.

Mr. Montgomery stepped down as Rudy took the mic. "Ladies and gentlemen, I'm very sorry to tell you there's been a slight change of plans. We won't be able to take any questions this evening."

A disappointed groan rippled through the crowd.

"I know. Thank you again." He skittered down from the stage and joined Sammy and Rob just as they were getting Mr. Montgomery to the back door.

"I can stay here for a while to make sure things settle down," Sammy said, opening the door. Red and blue lights flickered against the building across the alley, letting her know that Jones and his men had finally showed up. "And someone will have to lock the place up."

"That should be fine," Rob agreed, "if you're sure you can handle it. I'm worried about that crowd in there, though, and—" He stopped talking and his footsteps halted on the gravel of the alley.

Sammy nearly ran into him. "What is it?"

"Oh, not again!" Rudy whined.

The car Mr. Montgomery had rented in town—saving the limo service and the expense of it for grand entrances—had been vandalized. Someone had keyed the side of the car, leaving long scratches in the doors. The tires had been punctured, the black rubber flattened against the ground. On the back windshield were words written in spray paint, 'I'll Tell Everyone!'

Rob was quick to act. "We'll take my car instead."

"I'm sure it's still drivable," Mr. Montgomery hedged.

"Maybe so, but there's no telling what else someone might've done to it. What if they cut the brakes or something? You're not getting in that car." Rob took the old man's elbow and began leading him just around the corner of the building.

"Besides," Rudy took up the argument as he followed them, "just think of what it would do to your publicity to get into a vehicle decked out like that? We don't need to advertise these sorts of things…" His voice trailed off as he headed to Rob's car.

Sammy pursed her lips at the damaged vehicle. Why were the people of Sunny Cove so upset about this man? Mr. Montgomery seemed like a great guy to her. Sure, he was a little picky about the hotel, but that wasn't the sort of thing that made people stage protests or destroy a car. In fact, Sammy doubted the public even knew about that aspect of Mr. Montgomery's personality. The only reason she knew about it was because she'd happened to overhear his conversation with Rudy, and Tim from the Logan Hotel had told her what a difficult guest he'd been.

Sheriff Jones came through the back door, looking around until he saw her standing near the car. "We got here as soon as we could, but I guess we were too late," he said grimly, taking in the damage.

Sammy pulled out her cell phone and took a picture of the car. "Maybe, but there's no telling exactly when this happened. Rob and Rudy already took Mr. Montgomery back to the hotel in Rob's car. What about the protestors?"

"They scattered as soon as they saw us. I caught sight of a few faces, but nobody I recognized. I'd say someone is very much against this man making governor." He crossed his arms in front of his chest. "What do you make of it?"

"I don't really know yet." She felt like she was disappointing the sheriff by saying so, but it was the truth. "I do think it's interesting that the handwriting on the car is different from that of the note."

"Yeah?"

"Mmhmm. I mean, it's spray paint in this case, so that would account for some of it, but the lettering here is much more blocky."

Jones tweaked up one corner of his mouth in a half-smile. "Looks like I gave the case to the right detective."

"I don't know," she hesitated. "It's not like I have other handwriting samples to check out. I can't canvass the whole town and make everyone write for me."

"Maybe not, but I have a feeling you'll come up with something. And I hate to say it, but Rudy was right about getting fingerprints off the brick. We couldn't get anything worth using." His phone rang just then, and he pulled it from his pocket.

"Jones here." He pulled the phone from his ear to save himself from the screaming voice at the other end. Sammy couldn't understand the words, but she could definitely hear the anger flowing through the phone. The sheriff remained calm. "I think what you need to understand, Mr. Rush, is that you and your candidate aren't the only people in town. I can't prevent every single crime. And if you're so concerned about security, then maybe you should hire your own people." He hung up and put the phone away. "I guess our friend is a little miffed at me."

Sammy sighed. Things were only getting worse. "I'd better get back inside and make sure nobody is destroying the place." She headed in the back door, ready for a long evening of cleaning up the mess left behind by Montgomery's supporters.

8

DETECTIVE SAMMY BAKER, ON THE CASE

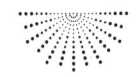

"You sure you're up for company?" Heather asked as Sammy let her in the front door. "You look like you could go to bed and sleep for a week."

"That sounds heavenly," Sammy agreed. "I've hardly even had time to work because I've been so busy working with Mr. Montgomery. Of course, Helen has been nice enough to let me take several days off, but I still feel bad about it. And it definitely hasn't been all sunshine and rainbows." She'd done her best to pamper herself a little bit, soaking in a warm tub and then putting on her most comfortable sweats, but she still felt exhausted.

"So then back off a bit," Heather offered as she sat down on the sofa. "You don't have to sacrifice everything you want or need just to make someone else happy."

"When did you become a lifestyle guru?" Sammy asked with a smile. "It's a great idea, but it's a lot harder than it sounds. I mean, this is the only time Mr. Montgomery is going to be here. I can't just back out of it now, not when he's encouraging everyone to donate to the homeless cause. This is a big opportunity."

"Yes," Heather agreed, "and the entire town has been turned on its head ever since."

"I can't argue with that, although I wish I could. The protestors that keep showing up are like ghosts. Nobody recognizes them, which means they're not from around here, and they disappear as soon as the authorities show up. That doesn't leave us much to work with."

"So what *do* we have to work with?" Heather asked, one eyebrow raised.

"You know, I was kind of hoping you'd say that," Sammy admitted. She got out a notebook and a couple of pens. "Jones basically told me he thinks I can figure out who's trying to derail Montgomery, but I haven't really had time to assess the situation."

Heather slapped the corner of the coffee table as she scooted to the floor. "Then I'd say it's time! Let's go!"

Sammy had helped the sheriff solve several crimes in the past, but it was even better when she had someone to do it with her. "I'll get us some hot chocolate. You know, to help us think."

A few minutes later, they began their work. "Okay, let's think about everything we've got," Sammy began. "We have a note and a brick that were thrown through the window of the hotel, and we have a vandalized car. Neither one of those acts were likely to be committed by someone who didn't know Montgomery's schedule."

"Not necessarily," Heather countered. "Anyone who knows the Logan Hotel would know where the presidential suite is, and it's a pretty easy guess that he'd be staying there. As for the car, if it has rental plates then it's obviously someone from out of town."

"Good point." Sammy tapped her pen on her chin. "Jones said they haven't been able to identify the protestors, though. That means they're not from Sunny Cove, so how would *they* know where the presidential suite is?"

Now it was Heather's turn to think, rapping her nails against the glass top of the coffee table. "What if one doesn't have anything to do with the other?"

"It seems more likely that they do, but I guess it's not impossible. The protests could be a completely separate thing."

"Have you asked Mr. Montgomery why anyone would be so upset with him?"

Sammy sighed. "I was going to, but Rudy threw a bit of a fit. He said talking about it really upset the old man, and I didn't want to be the one to agitate him. And Rudy said he had no idea why anyone would threaten Montgomery."

"Not helpful." Heather slouched back against the front of the couch. "You said you and Chelsea did a little research on him before he showed up in town. Did you find any dirt?"

Sammy snapped her fingers. "No, but we were only looking at the official fan page. Nobody would publish anything on there that wasn't pristine." She quickly pulled out her laptop, doing a general search instead of going directly to the authorized site. "Oh, look at this! He went through a messy divorce."

Heather leaned over to read. "He and actress Hannah Carlton split up back in the nineties, and the ordeal was on the front page of numerous tabloids and celebrity newspapers. She accused him of having numerous affairs."

"And she used that as leverage to get as much money out of him as possible, according to this article." Sammy shook her head. "It's hard to believe a sweet old man like that had been through a nasty divorce."

"Doesn't look like he ever got remarried, according to this. Do you think his ex could be responsible?" Heather mused.

Sammy pursed her lips as she opened a new tab and did another search. "She could be, but it would be pretty difficult considering she's been dead for five years."

"Okay. We can scratch that off the list!" Heather made a note on the pad. "Moving on. Any other scandals? Maybe from the women he supposedly had affairs with?"

Skimming the articles, Sammy tried to find something else noteworthy. "Doesn't seem like there's much. The only other thing I'm finding is that he had a falling out with a director back in the seventies, and the movie they were working on together never got made. Something called *No Ticket to Ride.* Other than that, looks like he's pretty clean. No time in jail, no rehab, none of the kind of stuff you normally hear about with celebrities."

"Huh. I'm stumped. How about you?"

Sammy sat back from the computer screen. "There's got to be something we're missing. I mean, what if Montgomery himself isn't the target at all? What if it's Rudy?"

"You think?"

"It's possible. I mean, neither the note or the message on the car were addressed directly to Montgomery, and Rudy is the only other person who's been with him the entire time." Sammy slid the notebook closer and wrote down Rudy's name.

"Building on that, what if it's neither Montgomery or Rudy? I mean, you and Rob have been around the whole time as well. Both of you were at the hotel and at SCS. Do you think there's still someone who's angry about the idea of the homeless shelter?"

Sammy frowned. "I hope not. I assumed we got that all cleared up when we proved that the homeless weren't the ones committing crimes, but I suppose there could still be an issue. The only thing that doesn't make sense about that theory is the fact that Rudy said these types of incidents were happening in other towns, as well. Rob and I weren't with them then."

The knock on the door startled Sammy, and her heart thundered as she got up to answer it. Heather's idea wasn't entirely off-base. What if it was the trouble maker coming after her?

But it was only Sheriff Jones. He was out of uniform for once, dressed in jeans and a baggy sweater. "Hey, Sammy. I haven't seen you very much lately except through a crowd of people, and—" He paused and coughed when he noticed Heather in the living room. "And, uh, I just thought I'd stop in to see what you'd come up with on the case."

Sammy opened the door wider to allow him in. "Actually, we were just working on that."

"Both of you?"

"Yes," Sammy said with a smile at Heather. "We make a pretty good team, and it's always nice to have someone else to bounce ideas off of. But you can sit down and join us. I'll make some more hot chocolate. " She headed for the kitchen.

"I'll join you," Heather said as she scrambled to her feet. "I need more marshmallows anyway." Once in the kitchen, she leaned close. "I don't think he's here to work on the case."

Sammy glanced toward the kitchen doorway, just to be sure Jones hadn't followed them in. "What do you mean? Of course he is."

But Heather's smile was smug. "Yeah, right. He hasn't seen you at all except through a crowd of people? No way, Jose. He's just jealous that you've been spending all that time with Rob."

"Stop it!" Sammy flicked her hand at Heather in an effort to shoo her out of the kitchen. "There's nothing like that between Rob and I!"

"Well, you know that, and I know that, but I'm not sure Sheriff McJealousPants knows that."

Pulling in a deep breath and letting it out slowly, Sammy did her best to put on a serious face. "There's nothing like that between Rob and I, nor is there anything like that between the sheriff and I. I'd appreciate it if we could all act like mature adults here." Inside, she was bursting with laughter and maybe a little bit of excitement.

"Okay, sure. But if you two decide you need your privacy you just give me the signal."

Sammy gave her a playful slap on the arm as the two women emerged from the kitchen, giggling.

9

A CRUCIAL INTERVIEW

Sammy, Heather, and Sheriff Jones had only managed to come up with a small list of suspects. They could've expanded on it quite a bit if they wanted to really reach out into left field, but Jones' presence had added an air of gravity to the night that had served to keep them on track.

So Sammy did her best to cross off whatever suspects she could, and she organized a dinner on the house at Just Like Grandma's for Cliff, Judy, and the others. It'd been her experience that these folks often had their ears to the ground when regular working stiffs were too busy to notice, and she hoped they could be helpful.

"It's nice to see you back behind the counter," Helen said with a grin as she flipped over the sign in the window. They were closed for business to the public, and that way the drifters wouldn't need to worry about being stared at. "We've sure missed you around here lately."

"And I've definitely missed the normal work schedule," Sammy admitted as she came around the counter to lay out plates and silverware at their biggest table in the corner. "Remind me never to get involved in politics again. It's running me ragged."

"But it's for a good cause," Helen reminded her. "I saw some of the footage from his speeches. He really wants to help."

"Yes, but if I could figure out who's trying to stop him, that would really help me."

Just then, Cliff walked in with Judy on his arm. Sammy could tell they'd done their best to clean up for the occasion, probably in a gas station bathroom, and her heart hurt for them. Carter and Cooper came in on their tail, along with several others. Buckets brought up the rear.

"Come on in and have a seat, everyone," Helen welcomed them warmly. "I'm just finishing up the roast, and we'll have it all out to you in a moment."

"I'm sorry it was such short notice," Sammy said as she greeted them. "I've been busy lately, and I hoped you'd be able to make it."

"Of course!" Cliff enthused. "Our schedule is pretty open!"

Judy gave her husband a wry look. "This was perfect timing, dear. Today is actually our wedding anniversary."

"It is? Did you hear that Helen?"

"I sure did. Sounds like we'll need to have some dessert to celebrate!"

Sammy and Helen sat down to eat with their friends, but they were the first to jump up as soon as anyone ran out of tea or lemonade or the gravy boat needed refilling. When they'd had their fill, they spread out a little to chitchat.

"What can you tell me about your friend over there?" Sammy asked Judy. "I see him at all the events and dinners, but he doesn't seem interested in talking."

She nodded. "He's more of a private sort. He does talk sometimes, but he seems very choosey on who he decides to converse with. I mean, we had a complete stranger walk into our camp several days ago, and Bucket sat up with him half the night. Don't take that personally, though."

"I won't." And she wouldn't, because she understood everyone was different. But something about that comment caught her attention. "What can you tell me about this stranger?"

Judy twisted up her face. "Not much. He claimed he was looking for someone to help him with a job. Cliff and I have been around long enough to know that it was probably some sort of scam, but we still let him share our fire. He and Buckets hit if off, but then the guy was gone the next day."

"And did he ever do this job?" This was getting stranger by the second.

She shrugged. "I don't really know. He didn't say anything else about it."

"You think it would be okay if I talked to him?"

"Sure, but I can't make any promises on whether or not he'll actually talk back."

Sammy headed over to the dinner table, where Buckets was still picking at his food. "Is everything to your liking?" she asked kindly.

He gave her a furtive glance before nodding.

Sammy slid into a chair across from him. "I wonder if you can help me with something."

Buckets pulled his head down and his shoulder up, shrinking into himself.

"It's not anything difficult, I promise. I just wonder if you can tell me about this stranger that came through town about a week ago." She kept her voice low, not wanting anyone else to overhear.

Now the homeless man had set down his fork and folded his arms stubbornly against his chest like an overgrown child having a tantrum.

"You see, someone hasn't been very nice to that politician that's visiting our town, and I'm trying to figure out who it is."

"What'd they do?" He'd muttered the words so quietly that it took Sammy a moment to decipher them.

"Well, someone threw a brick through his hotel window, and then—"

"I did it, okay?" Buckets shoved his dinner plate aside as he launched himself out of his chair. "I threw the brick! I didn't want to, but he said he'd give me a lot of money! And I needed the money! I'm cold, and I'm tired of being cold, but I don't want to go to jail!" The poor man had tears streaking down his dirty face now. He'd jumped to his feet during his outburst, but he crumpled back in on himself in fear. Cliff and Judy raced to his side, each putting an arm around him to calm him down.

"Nobody is going to send you to jail," Sammy reassured him. She was fairly certain she could work something out with Sheriff Jones, anyway. "But I do need you to help me a little bit more, okay? Can you tell me about the man who paid you to throw the brick?" She knelt in front of him, feeling terrible for causing him so much grief.

"He didn't pay me at all," Buckets wailed. "He said he'd come back and pay me, but he never did."

"I'm really sorry he let you down. Can you tell me what he looked like?"

Buckets sniffed. "He had a big nose and long hair down to his shoulders."

"Anything else? Do you remember what color his eyes were or anything?"

The poor man shook his head. "He wore these little dark glasses, even when the sun was gone."

"Thank you very much, Buckets. That man never should've asked you to do such a terrible thing, and

I'm sorry he took advantage of you. Tell me, did he have you do anything else?"

"No, and if I ever see him again, I'm going to give him a real what-for!"

Helen stepped up. "Why don't we all sit down for a nice slice of pie?"

Sammy did her best to paste on a happy face and not let on that her mind was whirling a million miles a minute. She'd discovered at least part of the answer to how the brick went through the window, but it didn't explain the car. She still had some work to do, but she was running out of time.

10

NEW EVIDENCE

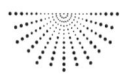

"You know, Rudy, I'm starting to think Sheriff Jones was right." Stephen Montgomery looked positively elegant in a wool suit and a dark red ascot, standing in the Sunny Cove Recreation Center with a glass of red wine in his hand. The swimming pool, separated from the rest of the building by a glass wall, cast dancing blue reflections throughout the room.

"Right about what, sir?"

"This whole security thing. Jones and his men have been all over the place this evening. Things have gone smoothly, but it doesn't seem very fair to expect them to do that all the time, and to expect it in every other town we visit." He sipped his wine and looked around the room.

"Their salaries are paid with taxes," Rudy argued, "and it's their job to protect everyone in the town!"

"Yes, but we can't expect them to act like bodyguards…"

Sammy's attention drifted away from the conversation. Mr. Montgomery was right. Things had gone smoothly, but too smoothly. The presence of the officers had kept any would-be protestors at bay. The vandalized car had been turned in along with a lengthy insurance claim form, and Rob and Sammy had been careful not to disclose Mr. Montgomery's exact plans or route once he left the Rec Center. The whole event was as safe as they could possibly make it without running background checks on every person in attendance, but Sammy had a feeling Rudy would take her up on that idea if she'd brought it up to him.

Still, she was just waiting for things to go wrong.

"You know, I'm starting to think that's something else I need to address in my speeches. We should utilize the services that our government pays for, but there's a difference between using them and taking advantage of them. I should make some notes for my speech, and it's just about time to start. Hold my drink, Rudy."

But as the campaign manager reached out for the delicate glass, he tripped over the carpeting. He launched forward, bumping the glass and spilling red wine all over Mr. Montgomery's crisp, white shirt. "Oh, no! Oh, dear! I'm so, so sorry!" He snagged a paper napkin from the refreshments table and dabbed uselessly at the stain. "I'm sure we can get this out."

"Not like that we won't!" The politician pinched the fabric and held it away from his skin.

Sammy could see that Mr. Montgomery was trying to keep his head, but he was having a hard time. "Listen, I can run back to the hotel and get another shirt for you. Rudy, I'm sure you can stall the crowd for a moment."

"I could just run back to the hotel myself..." Mr. Montgomery began.

"Don't you worry yourself over that. It'll be faster if I go, since I know this town like the back of my hand. I can take a few shortcuts and be there in no time. I promise, I'll hurry!" She dashed away from the two of them and found Rob near the front door. She quickly explained the situation to him before trotting out to her car.

Sammy hoped things didn't get too crazy while she was gone. Or maybe, she thought sarcastically, she was the problem. Maybe everything would go just fine as long as she wasn't in attendance. Either way, she knew she could zip back to the hotel faster than either Rudy or the elderly actor, and it was probably safer to keep Mr. Montgomery in one spot where they could keep an eye on him.

Sammy took a couple of back alleys to avoid long traffic lights and pulled up in front of Logan Hotel soon enough. She realized as she locked her car that she'd forgotten to get the room key from either of the visitors, but hopefully she could take care of that without having to return to the Rec Center. She burst through the front door and into the lobby.

The old hotel looked particularly beautiful in the late evening. The light fixtures still had the original glass globes on them, which cast a cozy glow on the pastel colors. If Sammy had the time, she would've loved to just plunk down in one of the overstuffed chairs and relax for a few minutes. Tim was behind the front desk, looking a little harried as he worked with a new software program that seemed in direct contrast with the atmosphere of the room.

"Tim! I need your help!" Sammy said breathlessly as she charged up to the desk.

His brow still furrowed from his work on the computer, he glanced up at her. "Sure. What's up?"

"I need to get into Mr. Montgomery's room. I know it's not the kind of thing you can normally do, but wine was spilled on his shirt at the Rec Center. I told him I'd run back here and get a new one, but I forgot to ask him for the key, and I've got to get it and get back there, and—"

"Whoa, whoa, whoa." Tim turned around and slid aside a wooden panel on the wall behind him. The shallow cabinet it revealed, held numerous hooks, many of them empty. He plucked a small gold key from the hook with the presidential suite's room number. "You're good to go. And enjoy that key, since they're trying to get the hotel switched over to electronic locks and key cards. I don't think that's going to sit well with the history buffs, though."

Sammy stared at the key in surprise. "Are you sure? I don't want to get you into trouble."

He waved off her concern. "If it were anyone else and any other circumstances, then things would probably be different. But I know you and Rob have been working closely with them. Besides, the sooner all this political stuff is over with, the sooner I won't have to deal with having bigwigs in the hotel. I actually had someone come in here and ask to put up a campaign flyer for the current governor."

"I'm sorry this has been so much trouble. I hope it's at least kept some rooms booked." Sammy had been hoping that Mr. Montgomery's visit would be truly good for Sunny Cove, but now she was beginning to wonder.

"Oh, sure. We've been full to the brim, so there's definitely not harm in that. In fact, I think we might even have some people who might come back to vacation here."

"That's wonderful, Tim. I'm going to rush right up, and I'll bring this right back to you." Clutching the key between her fingers, Sammy trotted up the stairs. Her thighs didn't burn the same way they had when Mr. Montgomery had first arrived, so at least she was getting some exercise.

The key fit solidly into the lock and she pushed the door open. Mr. Montgomery and his campaign manager were neat guests. Housekeeping hadn't come through to make the bed, yet, but the linens on the king-sized bed were tidily pulled up to the pillows. The cot Rudy was using was a bit more tumbled, but that was the only sign anyone had been in the room besides a pair of slippers lined up along the edge of the rug near the bed. The window was still boarded up, and Sammy guessed the hotel manager was waiting until the guests were gone to do the repairs.

She turned to face the wardrobe and dresser, and Sammy realized then she had no idea exactly where Mr. Montgomery had his shirts or which one he would want. She just had to do her best. She opened a door of the wardrobe and found a row of crisply pressed white shirts. She whisked one out and frowned. It was far too short for a man of Mr. Montgomery's stature. It had to belong to Rudy.

She put the shirt back and was just about to close the wardrobe when something caught her eye. Her heart thundered as she pushed the shirts aside to reveal a shoulder-length wig. Next to it was a rubber nose. Not the kind of nose someone might find in a cheap costume store for Halloween, but a good one made out of latex and with thin edges that could be covered up with makeup. Sammy's lips drew to a thin line as she opened the small drawer next to the row of shirts and found several little pots of flesh-colored makeup.

Terrified of what this all meant, she shut the wardrobe door solidly. She started to head for the door when she remembered the original reason she'd come here. Checking the dresser, Sammy found a well-organized drawer of shirts that were much more likely to fit the politician. She grabbed one and hurried back to the front desk.

"Get what you needed?" Tim asked as he took the key back.

She nodded grimly, feeling the rush of knowledge. It was almost overwhelming, and she had to figure out what to do with it. "I did. Thanks. I'll see you later." She headed back to the Rec Center, her head swirling.

11

CLOSING ARGUMENTS

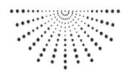

Sammy and Sheriff Jones sat in the farthest corner of the hotel lobby with their heads together. To anyone who happened to glance their direction, it may have looked like a romantic encounter as they whispered to each other, their eyes alight with anticipation. But Sammy and Jones both knew this was all about business.

"You really think this'll work?" Sammy asked, eyeing once again the satchel-style briefcase at his feet.

He nodded solemnly. "I think it's the best chance we've got. Anything else is going to take more time, and I don't know that we have it. I'm also glad that you're actually letting me get involved this time instead of trying to apprehend the perpetrator yourself." Jones gave her a sardonic smile.

"I could just go up there alone. I mean, you did practically hand me the case." Even though they were joking with each other, Sammy couldn't really blame him for the comment. She had a reputation of going too far on her own, especially since she wasn't officially employed by the sheriff's department. And she may have done the same this time, except this was a much higher profile case that involved a little more delicacy than just confronting the suspect.

Jones checked his watch. "If you're good, I say we go get this over with."

She nodded and stood, smoothing her dress pants and sweater. This might be the very last day that Montgomery would be in town, but she still wanted to look professional. "Let's do it."

Their footsteps echoed heavily on the wide staircase, and Sammy felt every thump of her heart as they approached the presidential suite. Sammy rapped on the door.

Rudy opened it a moment later, his eyebrows lifting when he saw them. "Stephen, it's Miss Baker and Sheriff Jones."

"Well come in, come in! I was just telling Rudy it was time for us to get off our lazy rumps and get packing. We've already stayed a little longer than we'd originally planned, and I don't want to disappoint anyone in the next town."

"I don't want to interrupt what you need to do," Jones said as he tugged on the brim of his hat in greeting, "but we thought we'd go over a few things with you. We may have some new developments when it comes to this whole messy situation."

"We?" Mr. Montgomery questioned as he stood up from the little seating area to the right of the bed. Half a cup of coffee and the remains of a croissant were on the table. "I must have missed something. I was under the impression that Miss Baker was an advocate for the homeless."

"She's very much that," Jones assured the politician, "but in a small town like Sunny Cove we know it's in our best interest to work with everyone in the community. In fact, if it weren't for Miss Baker, we might not've received some of our most intriguing testimony."

Mr. Montgomery sat back down and gestured for the two of them to join him. At his command, Rudy sat down as well. "Really? I'm listening."

This was Sammy's cue. "As you know, I work closely with the homeless population in Sunny Cove. I like to think many of them have even become my friends. What I noticed when Rob and I took you to meet them was that they were all very enthusiastic about your presence here except for one man."

"Ah, yes. The gentleman behind the dumpster. I remember. Are you telling me he was the culprit?" Mr. Montgomery sipped his coffee.

Sammy tipped her head to the side. "Not exactly. You see, I asked him about his behavior toward you, and he confessed that he did throw the brick through the window."

"Aha!" Rudy trumpeted, one finger in the air. "How terrible is that, sir, that the very people whom you're trying so hard to help are thwarting your efforts!"

"Hold on, before you jump to any conclusions," Jones warned softly. "The homeless man did throw the brick, but he did it because he was promised a tidy sum to do it. Both the brick and the note were provided to him by a stranger who came through their encampment."

Montgomery's gray brows drew together. "And did this man vandalize the car as well?"

"No," Sammy replied. This was the one piece of the puzzle she'd yet to figure out, but she hoped they had enough of them in place to still see the whole picture. "We explored as many options as possible with that, but we didn't come up with much, I'm afraid. There aren't any cameras watching the alley behind Sunny Cove Services, and nobody has come forward with any information to help the case. And we haven't been able to get a positive identification on the man Buckets spoke to. We only know that he had long hair and a sizable nose."

"I think it's safe to say that the same man who paid Buckets to throw that brick is probably behind the damage to the car. He keeps himself out of trouble by paying others to do the dirty work for him, and I wouldn't be surprised to find out that he'd paid those protestors as well." Jones was watching the two men carefully.

"Interesting," Mr. Montgomery mused, resting his chin on his fist.

"It's not interesting. It's despicable!" Rudy cried. "This has got to be someone from the governor's camp. They're worried you're going to win the election. They'll do anything to ruin your reputation, even lowering themselves to paying off the homeless and creating a scandal!"

"You know, Mr. Montgomery, you're very lucky to have someone like Rudy to run your campaign,"

Sammy said. "I don't know a whole lot about politics, but it's become very clear to me that Mr. Rush cares a lot about what happens. He's worked very hard to put on a good show during the time you've been here in Sunny Cove."

"Well, thank you very much," the candidate said proudly.

"In fact, he may have put on an even better show than you realize," Sheriff Jones said as he opened the briefcase and pulled out a clear evidence bag. Inside were the wig and the fake nose. "I mean, it involves costumes and everything."

Rudy's face visibly paled as he stared at the items. He swallowed twice before he spoke. "I'm afraid I don't completely understand."

Montgomery leaned forward, his elbows on his knees, looking back and forth between the evidence bag and his campaign manager. He was suddenly not an aging politician but a man of authority. "I'm afraid I don't either."

"This," Jones swung the bag a little, "was found right here in this room. And it appears to match the description of the man who said he would pay Buckets to throw the brick."

"And just what are you accusing us of?" Rudy said, straightening his shoulders and jutting out his chin. "You think we'd do this ourselves?"

Jones shrugged. "Well, Rudy, as you know, us small-town departments don't have all the sophisticated CSI equipment that the big cities do. But with a little bit of time, I'm sure we can send it off to a lab and have it analyzed. Of course, I'll need some hair and fingerprint samples from each of you so we can discern the culprit's DNA from yours."

Montgomery looked appalled, but he was still willing to cooperate. "Absolutely! The sooner we get to the bottom of this, the better. I'll cancel my next event if I need to. Should we go down to your station? Rudy, call the people in Evansville and tell them we'll be late."

But Rudy was sitting with his head in his hands. "Fine. I see. You two are slick. Stephen, the wig and the nose are mine."

"But why?" the actor demanded, his age-spotted fingers curling into a fist on the upholstered arm of the chair. "Why would you do such a thing?"

Rudy looked at him angrily. "You've been touting your time on the streets as your reason to help the homeless. But I happen to know you never had a rough day in your life."

"Excuse me?"

The campaign manager was growing indignant. "You even had me put that picture of you in a cardboard box up on your fan site, but that was just a shot from the set of *No Ticket to Ride*. The film was never made because you got into an argument with the director, and then you used that photo to launch a political career for yourself."

The old man's lips twitched as he tried to find the right words. "How do you even know that?"

"You forget that I'm *from* Hollywood. My mother was a makeup artist, and my father was a director. In fact, he was the director of *No Ticket to Ride*. He thought it would be his big break, but the producer canned the whole thing once you were off the project."

Sammy sat fascinated as all the details finally came to light. "So you waited all this time to get your revenge? Why even bother?"

Rudy looked more exasperated the longer this went on. "You ruined my father's career, and I carry the same name. I never could break into the business the way I wanted to. I figured I could either ruin your career as governor, or I could ride your coattails to a better job for myself if things didn't go as planned."

"So you've been paying people in every town to ruin all these speaking events?" Sheriff Jones asked.

"Yes," Rudy admitted grudgingly.

"I'm pretty sure there's not a good career in sabotaging political campaigns, Rudy. Let's head on down to the station."

12

A DOSE OF HONESTY

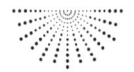

"This is quite the turnout," Mr. Montgomery said to Sammy as they peered over the railing into the lobby of the Logan Hotel. "I don't suppose I could engage you and Mr. Hewitt as my new campaign managers, could I?"

Sammy laughed. "A flattering offer, but I've decided I have no place in politics. It's too complicated. I just want to take care of my town."

The older man nodded. "An admirable goal. And given all those news cameras, I hope we can draw some attention to the real issues here in Sunny Cove. It's the least you deserve after putting up with me."

"Don't say that. It's been an adventure, and everyone needs that sometimes." She could see how this adventure had changed them all a little bit, especially Mr. Montgomery. He was quieter, more thoughtful, and Tim had reported to Sammy that the old man hadn't complained about a single thing ever since his stay in Sunny Cove had been unexpectedly extended.

"Shall we?" he held out his elbow to escort her down the stairs and to the stage that had been once again erected in the lobby, this time surrounded by news cameras and reporters.

"Thank you all so much for coming here today," Mr. Montgomery began. "I want to apologize to every single one of you, and while I wish I could do it individually, it'll be much faster if we can do it all at once."

A ripple of laughter flowed through the crowd.

"I've been misrepresenting myself during my campaign. I was never homeless, and the pictures you've seen of me in that state were from a movie set. I never should've lied, and having yet another lying politician isn't going to do myself or you any favors. But the truth is that I truly do care about the homeless. I'm not a perfect man, and I don't have all the answers, but I do still want to work with the rest of the state government to find the solutions."

Sammy smiled next to him. Mr. Montgomery might have lied, but his intentions were still good. It wouldn't have really hurt anyone if the truth about his time "on the street" had never come to light, but it was best that it had. And it was also good to know that Rudy Rush was safely tucked away in a cell, where he could no longer take advantage of the homeless community. Once he and Sheriff Jones had gone to the station, Rudy had admitted to ripping off many other people just like Buckets along the campaign trail.

"I know that I can't expect you all to simply accept my apology," Mr. Montgomery said, "but I would like to do something to prove to you that I really do want to make a difference. That's why I'm presenting this check from my personal funds for fifty-thousand dollars to Miss Baker and Mr. Hewitt, to help them make their dream of a homeless shelter in Sunny Cove come true."

Sammy gaped at him for a long moment, hardly even registering that he was holding out a check. She then remembered that everyone in the tri-state area was probably watching, and she accepted the payment and shook his hand. Unable to hold her excitement in, she threw her arms around Mr. Montgomery and hugged him.

When the news conference was over, Sammy waited for the crowd to die down before she found Sheriff Jones.

"Looks like you have plenty of work ahead of you, now that you've got some funding," he said with a smile.

She fingered the check in her suit jacket, still unable to quite believe it. "I do, but there's something I have to do first."

"What's that?"

She pulled in a deep breath. "I owe you an apology. When Rob and I first starting talking about Mr. Montgomery coming to town, you had your doubts. It caused nothing but chaos here. It turns out, you were right. I'm really sorry we put you through so much trouble."

His dark blue eyes twinkled at her. "Trouble is my job, Sammy. And if you hadn't gotten tangled up in this campaign, the truth might never have come to life. Rudy would still be out there taking advantage of people and causing damage to everyone and everything around him. And you definitely got what you needed for your shelter."

"Yes," she had to agree, her smile completely taking over her face. "We sure did."

~

THANK YOU FOR CHOOSING A PUREREAD BOOK!

We hope you enjoyed the story, and as a way to thank you for choosing PureRead we'd like to send you this free Special Edition Cozy, and other fun reader rewards…

Click Here to download your free Cozy Mystery
PureRead.com/cozy

Thanks again for reading.
See you soon!

OTHER BOOKS IN THIS SERIES

If you loved this story why not continue straight away with other books in the series?

Dying For Cupcakes

Rolling Out a Mystery

Christmas Puds and Killers

Cookies and Condolences

Wedding Cake and a Body by the Lake

A Spoonful of Suspicion

Pie Crumbs & Hit and Run

Blue Ribbon Revenge

Raisin to be Thankful

Auld Lang Crime

Stirring Up Trouble

Haunts & Ham Sandwiches

A Final Slice of Crime

OR READ THE COMPLETE BOXSET!

Start Reading On Amazon Now

OUR GIFT TO YOU

AS A WAY TO SAY THANK YOU WE WOULD LOVE TO SEND YOU THIS SPECIAL EDITION COZY MYSTERY FREE OF CHARGE.

Our Reader List is 100% FREE

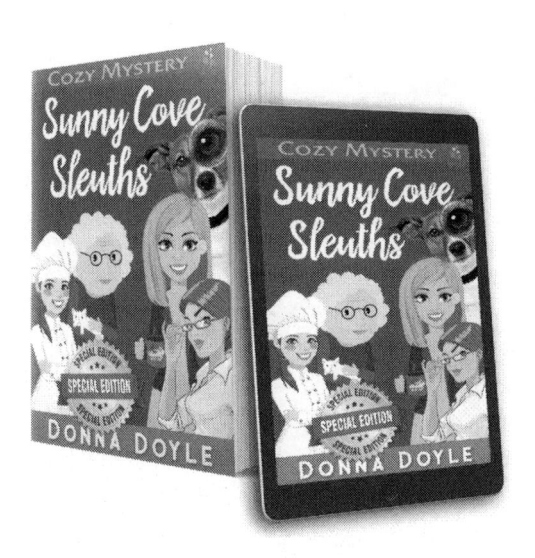

Click Here to download your free Cozy Mystery
PureRead.com/cozy

At PureRead we publish books you can trust. Great tales without smut or swearing, but with all of the mystery and romance you expect from a great story.

Be the first to know when we release new books, take part in our fun competitions, and get surprise free books in your inbox by signing up to our Reader list.

As a thank you you'll receive this exclusive Special Edition Cozy available only to our subscribers...

Click Here to download your free Cozy Mystery
PureRead.com/cozy

Thanks again for reading.
See you soon!

Made in the USA
Columbia, SC
18 February 2025